Read all the Commander in Cheese adventures!

COMMANDER IN CHEESE

3

Have a Mice Flight!

Lindsey Leavitt • illustrated by AG Ford

A STEPPING STONE BOOK™

Random House 🏠 New York

Text copyright © 2016 by Lindsey Leavitt, LLC
Cover art and interior illustrations copyright © 2016 by AG Ford

Photo permissions: pp. 84–89, 90, 93 from the collection of the Library of Congress Prints and Photographs Division online at loc.gov; p. 91 from the George Bush Presidential Library and Museum; pp. 95, 96, 97 from the collection of the Federal Government at wikimedia.org

Visit us on the Web!
SteppingStonesBooks.com
randomhousekids.com

Educators and librarians, for a variety of teaching tools, visit us at RHTeachersLibrarians.com

Library of Congress Cataloging-in-Publication Data
Names: Leavitt, Lindsey, author. | Ford, AG, illustrator.
Title: Have a mice flight! / Lindsey Leavitt ; illustrated by Ag Ford.
Description: New York : Random House, [2016] | Series: Commander in Cheese ; #3 |
"A Stepping Stone Book." | Summary: Ava and Dean Squeakerton, mouse siblings who live in the White House, hatch a plan to fulfill Ava's dream of flying by sneaking aboard Air Force One, the president's airplane.
Identifiers: LCCN 2015038759 | ISBN 978-1-101-93118-9 (paperback) |
ISBN 978-1-101-93119-6 (hardcover library binding) | ISBN 978-1-101-93120-2 (ebook)
Subjects: LCSH: Air Force One (Presidential aircraft)—Juvenile fiction. | CYAC: Air Force One (Presidential aircraft)—Fiction. | Flight—Fiction. | Mice—Fiction. | Brothers and sisters—Fiction. | Presidents—Family—Fiction. | White House (Washington, D.C.)—Fiction. | Humorous stories. |
BISAC: JUVENILE FICTION / Animals / Mice, Hamsters, Guinea Pigs, etc. |
JUVENILE FICTION / People & Places / United States / General. |
JUVENILE FICTION / Humorous Stories.
Classification: LCC PZ7.L46553 Hav 2016 | DDC [Fic]—dc23

Printed in the United States of America
10 9 8 7 6 5 4 3 2 1

This book has been officially leveled by using the
F&P Text Level Gradient™ Leveling System.

To MacKay, Emilia, and Miles
Dream big, small,
and all the spaces in between

★ ★ ★ ★ ★ ★ ★ ★ ★

Humans think they're the only dreamers in the animal kingdom. This is not true. All animals dream. And not just nighttime dreams—day dreams too. Yes, humans dream about bigger things. They want to ride unicorns or find pots of gold.

Animals are much simpler. Here are some common animal dreams:

1. Dogs dream about fetching a stick.
2. Chickens dream about crossing a road without humans making jokes about it.

3. C-a-t-s dream about ruling the world because they are evil.
4. Pandas dream about bamboo. And more bamboo. And more bamboo.
5. Sloths dream about . . . nothing. Well, they dream about more sleep. Sloths can be pretty boring.

Mice are smart animals, and so they have smart dreams. Ava Squeakerton wanted to do more than just look for cheese all day. Ava wanted to fly in the air. For many mice, making this dream come true would be very hard— mice don't have wings or money to buy airline tickets.

The Squeakerton family had lived in the White House for over two hundred years. Ava and her brother, Dean, knew they were very lucky to live in such an important building.

There was always food. They had Gregory, their Secret Service mouse, to look after them. And they were a part of history!

Ava and Dean were happy little mice.

Still, Ava would sit on the White House roof and dream her big dream. She could watch the birds fly overhead, but she never talked to them. Some birds ate mice. She didn't want her first time flying to be in a bird's mouth.

Ava tried to brainstorm ideas with her brother.

"What if we parachuted?" she asked Dean.

"What if we made a trampoline blanket?" she asked Dean.

"What if we rolled around in feathers?" she asked Dean.

What if, what if, what if. None of Ava's plans ever seemed to work. But Ava just wasn't thinking big enough. She didn't need to jump off a building. The most important plane in the world was within her reach.

Air Force One. The president's plane.

This is the story of how Ava and Dean got on that plane. The big question is, would they ever get off?

Ava and Dean had lived in the White House for a very long time—their whole lives actually. They'd seen all sorts of important people walking around their house. Royalty, actors, and athletes all wore very fancy shoes. There weren't a lot of kids walking in the halls, though. Adults did all the important human jobs, and the White House invited all the important humans.

President Caroline Abbey had two children, Macey and Banks. Macey was nine, and Banks was seven. The president's kids were very excited about their new home. They wanted to explore everything! This might not seem like a problem, but it was.

"Where are Macey and Banks today?" Ava asked Gregory.

Gregory looked at a clipboard. "The better question is, where *aren't* they? They've been in the bowling alley, the movie theater, the pool, and the kitchen."

"So we can't go anywhere?" Dean flopped onto a couch. They were in the common room, a very large room hidden in the walls of the White House. This was where the mice came to relax or play. Dean and Ava liked exploring better.

"You can't go in a room when the kids are there," Gregory said. "Your aunt Agnes has tried to create a pattern of their movements, but human kids can be very wild."

Ava twirled her tail. "Yesterday, the kids played hide-and-seek around the whole house, and we couldn't go anywhere."

"So?" Gregory said. "One hundred years ago, your ancestors didn't even have electricity!"

"Mice have bad eyesight. We use our whiskers. So what do we need electricity for?" Dean asked.

Ava sighed. "Look, Gregory. We just want to go in the movie theater for a little while."

"See! You want to use electricity." Gregory glared at Dean before checking his clipboard. "Movie time is at five today. You can go in there then."

Dean pouted. "But I'm bored."

"Bored? BORED?" Gregory roared.

Bored was not a word you used around Gregory. He tried to erase boredom. How did he do that? By doing more boring things.

"If you're bored, you can clean the common room. You can organize the Treasure Rooms. You can read history books and learn that little mice used to have to *work* around here!"

"I'll go do my homework," Dean said. "Come on, Ava."

"That's what I thought," Gregory said. "BORED? You live in the White House!"

Ava and Dean hurried out of the room and down a tunnel. If they didn't get away from Gregory, he might go on all day.

"Let's just peek into the movie room," Dean said. "If the president's kids aren't in there, we can stay."

"But that room isn't on the mouse schedule right now," Ava said. "It's out of bounds."

"When has that stopped us before?" Dean hopped through a mouse hole.

It was true. Ava and Dean loved adventure. They would stay safe. If they didn't, Gregory would find them.

Someone had left a movie playing. It was a cartoon about talking animals. What a great surprise! Ava and Dean ran around the room looking for treats. They found hard candy and popcorn on the floor.

"Jackpot!" Ava said.

Dean nibbled on a kernel. "And Gregory thought this wasn't safe."

The door to the theater room opened. Ava and Dean ran into a mouse hole.

The mice could see feet. Kids' feet.

"Oops. We left the movie on," Banks said.

"Where are the lights in here?" His sister, Macey, turned on the lights. "I need to find my backpack so we can go."

Ava and Dean paused. The kids were just stopping in the room for a little while.

"Let's wait a bit," Dean said. "We can grab those snacks after they leave."

"Okay," Ava agreed. "Too bad they're turning off the movie. It looks like a good one."

"Ugh, my backpack isn't in here!" Macey threw up her hands. "I bet it's in my bedroom."

"You leave that backpack everywhere," Banks said. "We have to hurry."

Macey smiled. "I know. It's our first time on Air Force One. I can't wait to tour the airplane!"

The kids left, and Dean hurried back into the room. "I wonder if there's any chocolate left over. They keep the White House so clean, it's hard to find good floor snacks."

Ava did not follow her brother. Ava did not move. She could not believe what she had just heard. Macey was going to tour Air Force One. The president's plane! This was Ava's chance. Finally.

"Uh . . . I gotta go. Bye!" Ava was too excited to tell Dean what she was thinking. Plus, she didn't want him to say no to her plan.

"Wait . . . Ava!" Dean ran after his sister. He followed her down the tunnel. He followed her right into the kids' bedroom. Ava and Dean had been in there once before, but it was not a room mice usually visited.

"Ava! Where are you going?" Dean asked.

Ava jogged around the room. She looked under a bed. She climbed onto a chair. Finally, she smiled and hopped down.

"Macey is looking for her backpack. Macey is also getting on Air Force One."

"But . . . what does that have to do with you?" Dean asked.

Ava rolled her eyes. "Obviously, I'm getting in that backpack so I can go too. I've always wanted to see a real plane. This is my big chance!"

3

Get on an airplane? Had his sister gone crazy? Wasn't living in the White House a big enough deal? Now she wanted to leave?

"Ava, let's think about this," Dean said.

"I've thought about this a lot," Ava said. "I've thought about this my whole life! I've waited and wished and wished and waited. Now this is my chance."

"But . . . but . . ."

Ava pushed past her brother. Macey's red backpack was in the corner of the room. Ava unzipped the zipper and wiggled into the front pocket. No one ever really uses the front pocket, so it was a good place to hitch a ride.

"You can get in trouble." Dean twisted his tail. "Like serious trouble. Not just Gregory trouble. Like being-lost-forever trouble."

"Did someone say trouble?" Gregory ran into the room. He didn't look happy. Surprise, surprise. "Kids. Come on. If you're going to run through the tunnels, don't be so loud! I thought you were doing homework."

Ava waved at Gregory from the backpack. "Sorry, Gregory. I'm going on a mission."

"What kind of mission?" Gregory asked.

Before she could answer, the door clicked open. Gregory and Dean ran inside a shoe. Mice have to hide all the time. Sometimes they get sick of it.

"Oof, this shoe smells," Dean whispered.

"Oh good. My backpack is in here," Macey said. "Banks, go tell Mom I'm on my way. I need to brush my hair first."

Banks stomped out of the room. "Sisters are so bossy!"

As soon as Macey and Banks were out of the room, Dean and Gregory ran over to the backpack. "Ava! Ava! Come on. Get out."

"No way!" came Ava's muffled reply. "I'm getting on a plane. And you can't stop me!"

The bathroom door opened. Gregory and Dean took one look at each other and jumped into the backpack. Gregory had just zipped them in when Macey picked up her bag and started walking.

The mice squished together in the little pocket.

"I can't breathe," Dean whispered.

Ava tugged the zipper open a bit for air. "You didn't have to come. I would have been fine."

"Fine?" Gregory sputtered. "Do you know how dangerous this is? What kind of risk you just took?"

"No, but I bet you'll tell me." Ava rolled her eyes.

"I sure will," Gregory said. "We can get dropped. Smashed. Thrown in with the cargo. Eaten by traveling pets. Die from no air, food, water . . ."

Dean squeezed his sister's tail. "I don't think this is the smartest thing you've ever done, but I'm excited."

Ava clapped her claws. "Me too!"

They bumped against each other as Macey ran down the White House steps. They stayed quiet as they heard car doors open and Macey slid into the car.

"Ready to go?" the president asked her daughter.

"Yes! I'm so happy. How long is the drive?"

"We have a presidential motorcade, honey," the president said. "That's a whole line of cars. It shouldn't take long. We'll take Marine One back to the White House from Base Andrews."

Macey slid her backpack onto the floor of the limo. The three mice slid into each other.

"Your foot is on my face," Dean said to Gregory.

"Quiet!" Gregory hissed. "What do you think will happen if they find three mice in the car with the president of the United States?"

"They're taking a Marine One back!" Ava said. "That's the name of the president's helicopters. So a car, then a plane, then a helicopter. It's perfect."

The mice were not as comfortable as the humans on the drive, but they were used to dark and cramped spaces. Ava counted fourteen bumps in the road. After what felt like days but was probably only an hour, the car stopped.

"Here we are!" the president said. "Welcome to Andrews Air Force Base!"

"Andrews Air Force Base," Ava said. "This is very official. Very important."

"You live in the White House." Gregory straightened his tie. "Isn't that big enough for you? Why do you have to go on a plane too?"

"Because I'm a big dreamer," Ava said firmly. "We're already here, Gregory. You might as well learn to like it."

Macey lifted her backpack from the floor of the car. Ava waited until Macey had strapped it onto her shoulders before undoing the zipper a little bit so the mice could peek outside.

In front of them was a huge stretch of road. Dean and Ava had seen roads from the roof of the White House but not something that went on forever like this. Ava had read enough books about flight to guess that this was a runway.

Macey turned around to say something to her mom. This gave the mice a chance to view the other direction. They were by an airplane hangar, which is where airplanes are kept. Of course. This was a very large building because Air Force One was a very large plane. The white building was shaped like a hexagon with six sides and large columns on each corner.

"Don't we have to go through security?" Macey asked.

"There is lots of security," Banks said. "Graham said they even have a trained army dog sniff all the bags."

The mice did not like the idea of a dog sniffing them. Who does?

"The Abbey family won't have the same rules," the president said. "So I'm not sure if a dog sniffs us. My staff, the reporters, and the flight crew do have to go through a lot of security. Not just anyone gets to fly on here. Airplane safety is very important."

The president's family walked into the hangar. The air was cool, and everything was clean. The floor was shiny. The ceilings were so high you could hardly see the top. It was one of the most amazing sights the kids had ever seen.

"This is huge!" Banks said.

"I don't think we're in Kansas anymore," Macey said.

Banks and Macey lived in Kansas before they moved to the White House. Their mom was the governor there before she became president.

Kansas was very far away. Kansas was never this fancy either.

Two identical airplanes were parked inside, one with an open door and stairs. Both airplanes were white on the top and blue on the bottom, with UNITED STATES OF AMERICA written on the side in bold letters. The presidential seal was also painted on the side.

Dean tugged on Ava's tail and pointed at the second plane. "Why are there two planes?" Dean asked.

"Air Force One is the name of any plane flying the president," Ava said. "There are two planes used as Air Force One."

"Huh. We should have two White Houses," Dean said.

Gregory snorted. "Two White Houses. Ridiculous."

The children wandered over to the front of the airplane. Macey ran her hands along the wheel. A group of men in suits stood behind them. When you're the president's kid, there are *always* men in suits around you.

"This plane is taller than the White House!" Banks said. "I can't believe you get to fly on these planes, Mom."

The president beamed at her children. "This job has its perks. Let's go inside. I'll give you a tour."

They walked up the stairs to the entrance of Air Force One.

"We have an hour," President Abbey said. "Let's explore."

"Can I take your bag?" a crew member asked Macey.

"Sure," Macey said. "Could you keep it close by? We're just looking around."

The backpack was set on a couch near the front entrance, so Macey could grab it when they were done with the tour. Once the humans left, the mice scrambled out of the backpack.

"Why couldn't she keep her backpack?" Ava asked. "I wanted the presidential tour."

"You just got a free ride to Air Force One," Dean said. "We are the luckiest mice in the world."

Ava did feel lucky. She had seen movies and TV shows with airplanes. She knew that on a regular flight, passengers entered the plane and smiled at a flight attendant. Then they found seats. That's what most planes are filled with—seats.

Ava also knew Air Force One was very

different. There were hallways. There were doors leading to rooms—an office, a conference room, even a bedroom for the president. There were two full kitchens. The colors were tan and brown, but it was still very fancy.

"Well"—Gregory hopped out of the backpack—"we might as well go meet the Mouse Corps."

"The Mouse Corps?" Ava asked.

Gregory had already jumped off the seat. Wait . . . Gregory was the one looking for an adventure?

Ava and Dean stared at him, openmouthed.

"Yes. The Mouse Corps. They should know we're here."

"But . . . but . . . don't you think we should stay by the backpack?" Dean asked.

"Do you want to see more of the plane or

not?" Gregory asked. "The president said we have an hour."

Ava readjusted her floppy aviator hat. You didn't have to twist her arm to see more of a plane! "Gregory, you're my new favorite mouse. Let's go meet the Mouse Corps, whoever they are."

5

Gregory, Ava, and Dean ran up the stairs and into the communication center. A woman in a blue flight jacket was talking on the phone. They waited until she turned. Then the mice slipped into a small hole in the corner.

"Here we are," Gregory said. "Welcome to the Mouse Corps."

"What is this place?" Dean asked.

The Mouse Corps command center was just underneath the top deck. Humans didn't know it existed. There were loads of buttons, TV screens, and speakers. Mouse-sized, of course.

Behind this was a lounge room with soft seats. Three mice sat on the ground, playing a game of cards. They nibbled on bits of fruit from a bowl.

One mouse stood up and shook Gregory's hand. "You must be Gregory. I'm Charlie. Welcome to Air Force One!"

Dean nudged Ava. They were thinking the same thing. Charlie did not look like someone who worked on a plane. He did not have on a pilot hat or jacket. Instead, he had on a backward cap and basketball shorts.

Gregory paused. "Um . . . so, you're the head of the Mouse Corps?"

Charlie saluted. "Yes, sir. I know, you probably expected a suit. But mice aren't supposed to be seen, right? So no one sees how we dress anyway."

"Well, yes, but dressing the part helps me take my job seriously," Gregory said.

"I understand," Charlie said. "It's different in the White House. In the Mouse Corps, there are only a few of us. So I tell all my mice to wear what they like."

This made a lot of sense to Dean and Ava. Gregory always wore a suit, so he probably didn't agree. The other mice waved. One lady had on a tutu and hiking boots. The other guy had on sunglasses and a Hawaiian shirt.

"Where did you come from?" Ava blurted out. "I mean, I didn't even know you existed!"

"Well, we know all about you, Ava and Dean Squeakerton," Charlie said. "You two are pretty

famous. For mice. Is it true you found a Lego for the Treasure Rooms?"

"Who told you about that?" Dean asked.

"Your dad. In his radio broadcast. Sometimes he tells stories about the other Squeakertons. We listen to a lot of radio here."

Ava's leg jiggled. She wanted to know all about the Mouse Corps. She wanted to *join* someday. "Um, can you please answer my question?"

Charlie laughed and led them into the break room. "Sure. As you know, the president's pilot goes through tons of training. He has to take many tests so he can fly such a special plane."

"Of course," Gregory said. "Everyone who works for the president is smart."

"It's the same for the Mouse Corps," Charlie said. "We're a group of mice from all over the country. These mice are very clever. We all have to find a way to D.C. to join the corps. Some mice hitch a ride on a train, or on a truck, or even in a suitcase. The mice have to be in good shape. They also have to learn everything they can about planes."

I can do all of that, Ava thought. If she studied hard in school and exercised and kept learning about planes . . . maybe . . . maybe this could be her job someday!

"Do you live here all the time?" Dean asked.

"We work in shifts on both planes," Charlie said. "Our home is built into the hangar, but of course we sleep and eat on the plane during very long flights. We radio in all the activity and news to your dad. Then mice around the country can know what is happening in the world. It's very important."

Ava nodded seriously.

Dean looked bored. "Did you say there's food on this plane?"

Charlie laughed. Gregory gave Dean a stern look.

Ava wanted to push all the buttons and spin in the captain's chair. She wanted to press her face against the little windows in the hall. Instead, she stared at Charlie. Creepy stared.

Charlie cleared his throat. "Any other questions?"

"Yes!" Ava bounced on her tail. "Do you help fly the plane? What does that green button do? How many miles an hour does this plane fly? What's the wingspan?"

Dean pinched his sister. "Ava, let the man speak."

Charlie grinned. "Your dad told me you love planes."

"My dad?" Ava asked.

Gregory rolled his eyes. "I radioed your father the second you little mice ran away. Remember, I'm always prepared. Always."

"Can I get a pair of wings?" Ava asked. "I mean, those little pins they give people on flights."

"Maybe. If you earn them," Charlie said.

Ava was just about to ask what the red light was for when it went off.

"That's weird," Charlie said. He stuck on earphones. The other members of the Mouse Corp hurried into the cockpit.

"What's going on?" Ava asked.

"They must have decided on a last-minute flight. The flight deck is preparing to leave."

"Like, into the sky?" Ava asked.

"Yep." Charlie took off his headset. "I'll have these guys listen to the radio for more information. Let's go spy on the humans. It's the best way to find out what's happening."

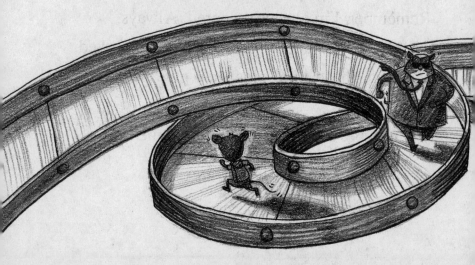

6

Ava, Dean, Gregory, and Charlie scampered down a mouse chute to the president's suite. The suite did not look like anything you might expect on an airplane. There were large white chairs, plush carpet, and soft music.

Macey and Banks were already in their seats.

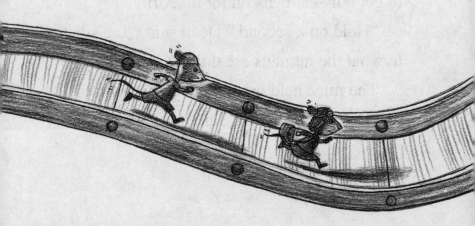

"Did you travel in the backpack?" Charlie asked Gregory, who was still cramped in the chute with Ava and Dean.

"Unfortunately," Gregory said.

"Well, you can't get back in there now. Not with the kids around."

The plane rumbled underneath them.

Charlie scanned the room. "Looks like we're starting to move. We should go."

Ava squeaked. "I wanted to watch through a window."

"We'll find you a window without humans once we're in the air," Charlie said. "We need to get our seat belts on for takeoff."

"Hold on a second," Dean said. "Let's listen to what the humans are doing."

The mice held on to the wall and waited.

"Do we get to eat on the plane?" Macey

asked the president, who sat across from her children. "I'm starving."

"Yes. You can order whatever you want," President Abbey said. "They have a chef. We'll probably eat when we're over Indiana."

"What do you mean, over Indiana?" Banks asked.

The plane rolled backward. Ava grabbed her brother's tail.

"I mean, we're taking a trip!" the president said. "I know you've been a little homesick since we've moved to Washington. So I'm taking you to Kansas to see your friends!"

"Home? We're going home?" the kids asked together. "There's no place like home!"

The mice had enough information. They started back up the chute.

The plane was going faster now. Ava could feel it under her feet. She didn't like that she couldn't see what was happening. She also didn't like the feeling in her stomach.

"I need to sit down," Ava said.

Charlie led the mice to the mouse lounge. They buckled into seats. The plane kept moving.

Dean asked Charlie all about the history of Air Force One. Charlie knew a lot. Even Gregory was impressed. Like, did you know Air Force One has nineteen televisions and eighty-five telephones? Isn't that interesting?

Ava didn't ask questions. Her ears felt funny. Ava did not get to watch the wings of the plane as they soared into the air. Even if there were a

window in the mouse lounge, it wouldn't have mattered.

Ava Squeakerton was feeling sick.

"Why aren't you paying attention to Charlie?" Dean asked.

Ava was about to answer. But instead, she threw up.

"**G**ross!" Dean yelled as Gregory handed Ava another barf bag.

"There's a bathroom down the hall," Charlie said kindly.

Ava wobbled out of the room. She washed her face and brushed her teeth. Charlie got her a ginger ale. She took deep breaths and tried to stop shaking.

"How do you deal with this feeling all the time?" Ava asked.

"You're airsick," Gregory said. "You've never flown before."

Dean made a face. "How does the mouse who always wanted to fly get *airsick*?"

"Remind me to aim for you next time I'm sick," Ava said.

Charlie took her tail. "Let's get you by a window. Then you'll feel better."

Charlie hurried Ava down a hallway and through a door.

"This is the medical room," Charlie said. "No one ever comes in here. Look—you can hop onto the seat and look out the window."

Ava climbed onto the seat. And then, finally, she looked out the window. She still felt a little sick, but the view definitely helped.

The sky had many different shades of blue. The clouds made a white blanket across the Earth. When Ava stared at the skyline, she felt less dizzy.

Ava was in the air. She was flying. This was a dream come true.

She closed her eyes, picturing clouds floating around her. And then . . . she took a nap. Ava slept through the very thing she'd waited her whole life to do.

The plane landed so smoothly, Ava didn't even wake up until Dean shook her.

"Come on, Ava! You slept for two hours."

Ava wiped drool off her mouth. "Really?"

"Really. Gregory and I already explored the cargo area, but now that the passengers are

getting off the plane, we can explore inside! Let's go."

Ava couldn't believe she had missed so much of the flight! At least she had seen through the window for a bit. She hoped she felt better when they flew back to Washington. She hopped off the seat with her brother, ready for another adventure.

8

The first stop for the mice was the kitchen. Dean had found a menu, and there was a leftover cheese plate waiting for him. And some mac and cheese. And a hamburger.

"If you were flying on almost any other plane, you wouldn't find food like this," Charlie said as he dug into peach pie. "They make all the food fresh in the air. The chef is wonderful."

"I'm just glad Macey ordered mac and cheese," Dean said as he swallowed another noodle. "These kids have great taste."

"Hey, this cheese is called Gruyère. That

rhymes with 'air.'" Gregory laughed. "We should call the plane Gruyère Force One!"

Ava and Dean shook their head. The only thing worse than Gregory being serious was Gregory trying to be funny.

"Don't be cheesy," Charlie said.

Ava didn't eat a lot. She was bummed she had missed so much of the flight. She was worried that she would always get sick like that. Then she could never join the Mouse Corps!

Gregory sat next to her and squeezed her tail. "I have a surprise for you."

"What, another barf bag?" Ava asked. "More cheese jokes?"

"No, this is even better. Come with me."

They left Charlie and Dean to their snacking. They left the whole second floor, actually, and slipped down a pole into the lower deck.

The cargo area of most planes is usually filled with luggage. There wasn't much of anything in this cargo area. That is because there are cargo *planes* that fly ahead of Air Force One. Yes, the president has a whole plane to carry cars and motorcycles! There is even a plane that pumps gas into Air Force One in the middle of flight.

Gregory opened a small hatch in the ground. Underneath was a tunnel that led to . . .

"A Treasure Room?" Ava asked in wonder.

The Squeakerton family had a whole series

of Treasure Rooms in the White House. Rooms filled with history. Rooms filled with family. The mice were very proud of their collection.

This room was not nearly as fancy. All the items were tied to the wall or hung from the ceiling. But that didn't matter to Ava. That little Treasure Room had loads of stuff to do with flight.

Here were just five items. . . .

1. A patch from Gerald Ford's flight jacket
2. A thirty-year-old bag of peanuts
3. A flight certificate for Socks, Bill Clinton's cat
4. Ronald Reagan's bathroom slipper
5. George H. W. Bush's old aviator hat

Gregory patted Ava on the back. "Did you know Christopher Columbus got seasick?"

"So?" she asked.

"So I bet he still loved ships and exploring. Getting seasick didn't stop him from discovering America."

"Are you saying this to make me feel better?" Ava asked.

"Is it working?" Gregory asked.

"Sort of," Ava said. "I guess . . . I guess the

exciting thing is . . . do you ever think I can be like Charlie? And work on a plane?"

Gregory shrugged. "Charlie isn't a Squeakerton. He's actually a Gunson, a mouse family that lives in the Empire State Building in New York. He somehow made it here and flies around the world."

"So it's still possible for me to be in the Mouse Corps?"

"For a mouse like you? Absolutely. You can be anything you want to be." Gregory cleared his throat. "Now, can we please go back before your brother eats all the presidential M&M's?"

Air Force One really did have its very own M&Ms that you can't find anywhere else in the world. Dean hadn't eaten all the M&Ms, but he had eaten plenty. He'd also asked Charlie question after question about living in a skyscraper. Dean loved buildings like Ava loved planes.

The president and her kids were just boarding the plane when the mice reached the hallway. The mice hid behind the couch.

"That was awesome, Mom!" Banks said. "Thanks for taking us to our old school."

"And to G's Frozen Custard," Macey said. "And our favorite BBQ place. The whole trip was so much fun."

Ava didn't even notice the problem until

Dean moaned. "Great. Now what are we going to do?"

"What are we going to do about what?" Ava asked.

"Uh . . . Ava?" Dean pointed at the humans. "Macey doesn't have her backpack."

He was right. Macey walked right into the president's bedroom without her backpack. Yes, the president has her own bedroom on the plane. Which is super cool. But stay focused on the fact that Macey kept forgetting her backpack!

Ava's stomach flipped, and this time she knew it had nothing to do with takeoff.

Gregory squeaked. Gregory might be a Squeakerton, but he was usually not much of a squeaker. "So . . . if Macey isn't carrying her backpack . . . how are we getting off this plane?"

Here are possible ways the mice could get off the plane and back to the White House:

1. They could run down the airplane stairs. But then they would be stuck in Kansas, which is very far from Washington.

2. They could run off the stairs after they landed in D.C. But then they had no way to get back to the White House. Maybe ever.

3. They could run into the car. But the

president said they were taking a
helicopter back to the White House.
There was no way they could get from
the plane to a helicopter without a human
seeing them. Do you know what a human
would do if they knew there were mice
on Air Force One? The answer involves
sad words like *traps* and *exterminator.*

4. They could . . . I don't know. Parachute?
Build wings? Drive a car? Look, these
mice did not have a lot of choices.

5. Um . . . do you have any ideas?

"But, Charlie . . . you get off the plane all
the time," Dean said. "So why don't we just do
what you do?"

"We *stay* in these planes," Charlie said. "Or
in the hangar. Even though we travel the world,

we don't usually see anything. I've never been to the White House, for example. It's dangerous, especially with this many humans."

Gregory sniffled. "That is so, so sad. The White House is the most beautiful building in the world."

"Gregory." Dean rolled his eyes. "Come on. We need a plan."

Ava and Dean had come up with plans before. And they would come up with plans again. They were a team, whether in the air or on the ground.

Charlie rolled out a piece of paper. Everyone brainstormed ideas. Some ideas were good. Some were very bad. Finally, they decided to go simple.

"We came on this plane in a backpack," Ava said. "So we just need to *leave* in something."

"Great, are you going back to Kansas to get the backpack?" Gregory asked.

Dean rubbed his chin. "Can we make an emergency happen in Kansas, like a flood? So then the president has to fly back. And while they're fixing the emergency, they can remember the backpack?"

When you are brainstorming, you never say an idea is bad. But . . . that idea was bad.

"We're not going to Kansas again, and we are *not* going to see that backpack. At least not for a long time," Charlie said.

"Okay. Okay." Dean tapped Ava on her elbow. "Come on, Ava. You've got this."

"We would . . . we would just have to leave on something they're wearing."

"Good idea!" Gregory said. "Way to put on your thinking cap."

Ava and Dean jumped up at the same time. "That's it!"

"What's it?" Gregory and Charlie looked confused.

"A cap!" Dean said.

"It's perfect," Ava agreed. "We get into a hat."

"But . . . neither of the kids are wearing a hat," Charlie said.

Dean hopped onto his other foot. "The kids aren't wearing hats *yet*."

"Yet? Yet? How are you going to change the 'yet'?" Gregory asked.

Ava and Dean were already running down the hall. They slipped through a hole and came right into the cargo area. Gregory and Charlie ran after them. Ava slipped into the Treasure Rooms and grabbed . . . the aviator hat!

"Found hat number one!" Ava said. "And look! It even has pockets in the flap!"

"We can't all fit in one hat," Gregory reasoned.

"Nope, that's the tricky part." Dean slapped Charlie on the back. "So, tell me, Charlie. How well do you know the pilot of the plane?"

"Mice aren't supposed to be seen *or* heard," Charlie said. "The humans can't know we're on the plane."

"Well, we need to get a pilot's hat," Ava said. "So that's the next part of the plan!"

The next part of the plan, of course, was the hardest part of all.

The good news:

- Air Force One has two pilots.
- Both pilots have a hat.
- The pilots don't always wear their hats.
- So those hats don't need to be borrowed from the top of their head.

The not-so-good news:

- The pilots didn't have twenty hats! If a hat went missing, they would notice.

- If the mice were lucky, the hats were kept in the pilot's flight bag.
- If the mice were *not* lucky, the pilots had left their hats at home.

"None of this would have happened if Macey would stop losing her backpack," Gregory muttered. "This whole plan could be a disaster!"

"Do you remember what President Ronald Reagan said?" Dean asked.

"Of course," Gregory said. "I remember what *all* the presidents have said."

"Then you know this quote. 'The future doesn't belong to the fainthearted; it belongs to the brave.'"

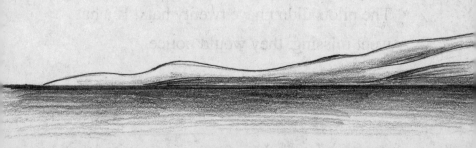

Gregory wiped at a tear. "Ronnie is right. Godspeed, soldier!"

Dean saluted. "Charlie! Blanket me!"

Charlie threw a blanket over the top of Dean. The plan was for Dean to very . . . very . . . very slowly move across the room under the blanket. If the hat was in the cockpit, Dean would take it.

"How are we going to make the kids wear the hat?" Charlie asked.

"We'll write a note. A really smart note," Ava said.

"I have perfect handwriting!" Charlie said.

"Great," Ava said. "You write the note. Gregory and I will look for a hat too."

By this time, the plane had already taken

off. The mice didn't notice. A full meal was served to the kids. The mice didn't notice. The kids watched a movie, and the president had an important meeting in her conference room. The mice didn't notice.

Each mouse was very busy doing their job. Let's check on Dean first. . . .

It took Dean an hour to move across the floor. He waited until one of the pilots got up to take a break, leaving the other pilot alone to fly the plane. The pilot was a good pilot and very focused on his job. *Gregory would like that about him,* Dean thought.

Dean peeked out from under the blanket. Dean did not like what he saw. There wasn't one hat in the whole cockpit. Now what?

Meanwhile, Ava and Gregory climbed through eight bags. They found an antique

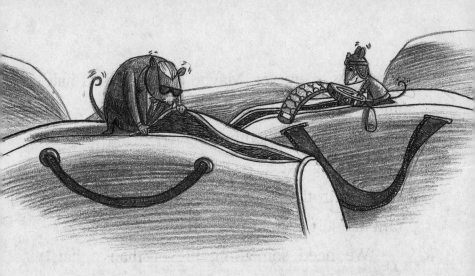

watch, a man's shaving kit, an old box of crack-
ers, and a worn stuffed elephant.

"But not one hat!" Ava said.

"So now what?" Gregory asked.

Charlie chewed on his pen. Macey's hair
was very pretty that day. When a human does
their hair a certain way, they don't want to cover
it with a hat.

"What if she isn't a hat type of girl?" Charlie
asked himself. These children were new. He did

not know them yet. Maybe one kid liked hats and the other one didn't!

"We need something bigger," Charlie said. "Something like a . . . jacket."

Back in the cockpit, Dean noticed the captain had left a flight jacket on his seat.

"We need something bigger than a hat," Dean said. "Maybe this will work out better."

Mice are very strong. Probably the strongest animals you will ever meet. Most humans don't know that, but that's because mice don't want them to know that.

So Dean picked up that flight jacket. No problem. He shoved it under the blanket and hurried across the floor.

The pilot walked into the room.

"You ready to take your break before we land?" his copilot asked.

The copilot yawned and stretched. "That'd

be great. Hey, is that your blanket on the ground over there?"

Dean froze.

"No. Maybe it's Jim's."

Dean didn't know who Jim was, but he sure liked Jim right then.

"Hey," the pilot said. "Have you seen my flight jacket?"

"You probably left it in the kitchen again," the copilot said.

"Yeah," the pilot agreed. "Probably."

Dean waited another five minutes, then hurried out of the room, the jacket dragging across the floor. He made it to the Treasure Room, where he waited for the other mice.

Meanwhile, back in the baggage area, Gregory and Ava gave up on finding a hat.

"I hope Dean found something," Gregory said.

"What about this?" Ava asked, holding up a beautiful scarf. Ava loved fashion and fabric. Scarves were her favorite.

"What will we do with that? Swing from it?" Gregory asked.

"I don't know," Ava said. "We can't go back empty-handed. Let's bring it just in case."

The mice met in the Treasure Room of Air Force One. When they saw the hat, the scarf, and the jacket together, they knew they had everything they needed to make their plan work. And there was still twenty minutes before they landed in D.C.!

"Let's go watch the plane fly!" Ava said.

They snuck into the president's office. Her spinning chair was one of the nicest ever. But the mice didn't spin. Ava stuck her face up to the glass of the window. They were still above the clouds. The wing was long and pointy.

"Charlie?" she asked.

"Hey, we should go buckle up before land-ing," he said.

"But, Charlie?" she asked again. "Do you think I earned my wings?"

"Oh, I think so."

Ava turned around to find Charlie, Greg-ory, and Dean holding a plastic pair of airplane wings. If flying was an ice-cream cone, this present was the cherry on top.

"It was so good to meet you, Charlie," Ava said.

"Yeah, you're really cool," Dean agreed.

"Don't worry, little mice." Charlie gave them both a high five. "I have a feeling we'll see each other again. Someday, somewhere."

"All right," Gregory said. "Enough with the goodbyes. Let's get off this plane. I miss the White House!"

11

Macey and Banks woke up from their naps just as the plane touched the ground. What a fun day! They got to fly on the most important plane in the world. But even better, they went home to Kansas to see their friends. Maybe someday their friends could visit them in the White House. Movie theaters were way more fun when you shared them.

The president hurried into the lounge. "Marine One is waiting for us. But first, come see this present."

Laid out on the president's bed was a flight

jacket, an aviator hat, and a scarf. Next to it was a mint and a handwritten note. It said:

Thanks so much for flying with us today! So glad to have you on board! Here's a little surprise for each of you to help you remember your first flight on Air Force One.

Best,
The crew

"This is so nice!" Macey grabbed the jacket just as Banks grabbed the hat. They looked at each other and laughed. "Guess this is the perfect present. Now who gets the scarf?"

The president wrapped the scarf around her neck. "You know, I have a scarf just like this one at home."

Or she had one in her flight bag. Or

she *did* have that very same scarf in her flight bag.

Photographers were waiting for the Abbeys at the entrance of the plane. The kids did not notice the three mice hidden in their hat or clothes. This was good, because Gregory was a big, heavy mouse.

"Madam President, can I take some pictures of you with your children?"

The family all beamed in their new clothes. The kids posed on the stairs. The pilots came out to shake their hands before the kids left. One pilot looked a little confused behind his smile.

"Hey," he whispered after the kids were off the plane, "was Macey Abbey wearing my flight jacket?"

The other pilot patted him on the back. "I think they thought those were gifts. We'll get you a new one. Wonder where Banks got that cool hat. President Bush used to have one just like it."

Marine One, the president's helicopter, was waiting just outside the hangar. The kids had never been in a helicopter! So much excitement in one day.

Ava and Dean squeezed hands in the chest pocket of the coat.

Ava's stomach flipped as the helicopter lifted into the air. The huge plane was smooth compared to this flight. Humans sometimes called helicopters *choppers* for a reason. Still, she was okay. She was more than okay. Her dream had just come true!

"Hey, Dean?" she whispered. "Guess what I'm thinking."

"That tomorrow we'll have to do something boring, like count the number of buttons in the Treasure Rooms."

"I've already done that. There's forty-eight," Ava said. "No. I think . . . I think I want to be in the Mouse Corps someday."

"Of course you do," Dean said. "You'll be great at it."

"You think so?"

"The Mouse Corps solves problems. You're

a good problem solver. Do you want to know what I'm going to do?" Dean asked.

"What?"

Dean wished he could poke his head out of the pocket. He knew that they were flying over D.C., and there were so many cool buildings. He wanted to see them all, far away and up close. Someday he would visit the Lincoln Memorial, the Capitol Building, and the Smithsonian. And someday after that, he wanted to go visit Charlie's family in the Empire State Building!

"I want to be an architect. And someday . . . I'm going to leave the White House and see all the beautiful buildings in the world."

"I can fly you there," Ava said.

"Sounds like a plan," Dean said.

"Hey, Dean? Let's not tell Gregory this plan."

Dean laughed. "No way. When we get back,

I'm sure he'll have enough chores to keep us in the White House forever."

Sure enough, Dean and Ava had to memorize the favorite foods of seven presidents as punishment for their adventure.

But even surer enough, they thought it was totally worth it.

The Presidents of the United States

George Washington
1789–1797

John Adams
1797–1801

Thomas Jefferson
1801–1809

James Madison
1809–1817

James Monroe
1817–1825

John Quincy Adams
1825–1829

Andrew Jackson
1829–1837

Martin Van Buren
1837–1841

William Henry
Harrison
1841

John Tyler
1841–1845

James K. Polk
1845–1849

Zachary Taylor
1849–1850

Millard Fillmore
1850–1853

Franklin Pierce
1853–1857

James Buchanan
1857–1861

Abraham Lincoln
1861–1865

Andrew Johnson
1865–1869

Ulysses S. Grant
1869–1877

Rutherford B. Hayes
1877–1881

James Garfield
1881

Chester A. Arthur
1881–1885

Grover Cleveland
1885–1889

Benjamin Harrison
1889–1893

Grover Cleveland
1893–1897

William McKinley
1897–1901

Theodore Roosevelt
1901–1909

William Howard Taft
1909–1913

Woodrow Wilson
1913–1921

Warren G. Harding
1921–1923

Calvin Coolidge
1923–1929

Herbert Hoover
1929–1933

Franklin D. Roosevelt
1933–1945

Harry S. Truman
1945–1953

Dwight D.
Eisenhower
1953–1961

John F. Kennedy
1961–1963

Lyndon B. Johnson
1963–1969

Richard M. Nixon
1969–1974

Gerald R. Ford
1974–1977

James "Jimmy"
Carter, 1977–1981

Ronald Reagan
1981–1989

George H. W. Bush
1989–1993

William J. "Bill"
Clinton, 1993–2001

George W. Bush
2001–2009

Barack Obama
2009–

Mice Are Smart!
Three Totally Cool Facts
About Presidents' (Other) Jobs

Like Teddy Roosevelt said, "Work hard at work worth doing."

1. Presidents are soldiers! Zachary Taylor served in the military for forty-one years. His victories in the Mexican American War made him a national celebrity and earned him the nickname Old Rough and Ready.

2. Presidents are architects! Thomas Jefferson said, "Architecture is my delight." He drew plans for government buildings, houses, churches, and the University of Virginia. It took him forty years to build his house, Monticello, which appears on the back of the nickel.

3. Presidents are pilots! George H. W. Bush was a naval aviator in World War II. He flew in fifty-eight combat missions and was awarded the Distinguished Flying Cross.

By Horse, Train, or Car—
These Presidents Went Far!

Safety first and always, little mice!

★ George Washington traveled by horseback during the Revolutionary War and his presidency. Along the way, he stayed in hundreds of houses and inns. "George Washington slept here" became a popular slogan for businesses.

★ When Lincoln was elected president, he took a twelve-day train ride from Springfield, Illinois, to Washington, D.C. This was called a whistle-stop tour because when the train stopped in many small towns, Lincoln gave speeches from train platforms, where trains blew their whistles.

★ William Taft was the first president to own a car in the White House. He changed the horse stables into a garage. His car was once hit by a trolley, causing the first presidential car accident.

Air Force One: Past

★ Theodore Roosevelt became the first president to fly in 1910 when visiting an airfield in Kinloch, Missouri. A pilot, who had just landed, asked if the former president would like to be a passenger. Teddy hopped right into the plane!

★ The first presidential plane, *Sacred Cow,* was made for Franklin Roosevelt and included an elevator for his wheelchair.

★ In 1962, President John F. Kennedy became the first president to fly in a jet built only for presidential use.

★ Like any airplane, Air Force One sometimes experiences rough flying. President Clinton was flying over Texas in June 1996 when the plane hit turbulence. The dinner enchiladas ended up splattered around the kitchen during this bumpy presidential flight!

★ At the Ronald Reagan Presidential Library in Simi Valley, California, you can tour the Air Force One Boeing 707 that flew presidents for twenty-eight years.

★ In 1947, President Truman replaced *Sacred Cow* with *Independence,* which was named after his hometown. The nose was painted to look like a bald eagle.

Air Force One: Present

★ Marine One is the name of any helicopter flying the president. There are thirty-five helicopters in the Marine One fleet.

★ The president has his own doctor on the plane whenever he flies. There is also a medical room in Air Force One.

★ The two kitchens on Air Force One serve gourmet food specially prepared by Air Force One's chef. The first meal President Obama ordered was a cheeseburger!

★ In case of emergency, Air Force One can be refueled by another plane *in flight*. No gas station stops needed!

★ The "beast" is the presidential limo, which drops him off and picks him up after flying. This car is transported on a separate cargo plane.

★ The next Air Force One is expected to cost roughly $3 billion to build and will be complete in 2023.

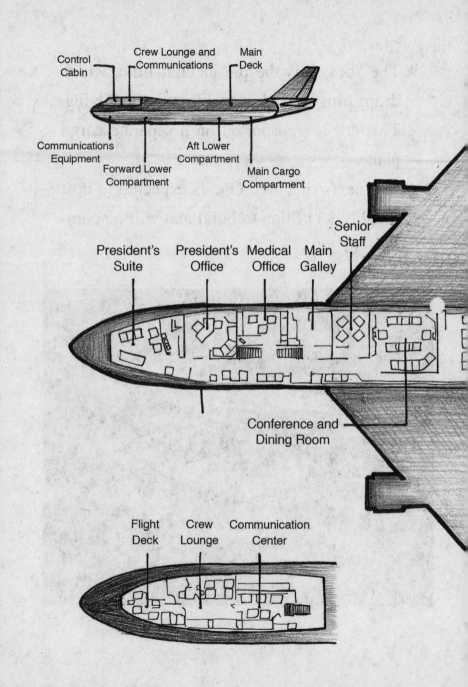

Control
Cabin

Crew Lounge and
Communications

Main
Deck

Communications
Equipment

Forward Lower
Compartment

Aft Lower
Compartment

Main Cargo
Compartment

President's
Suite

President's
Office

Medical
Office

Main
Galley

Senior
Staff

Conference and
Dining Room

Flight
Deck

Crew
Lounge

Communication
Center

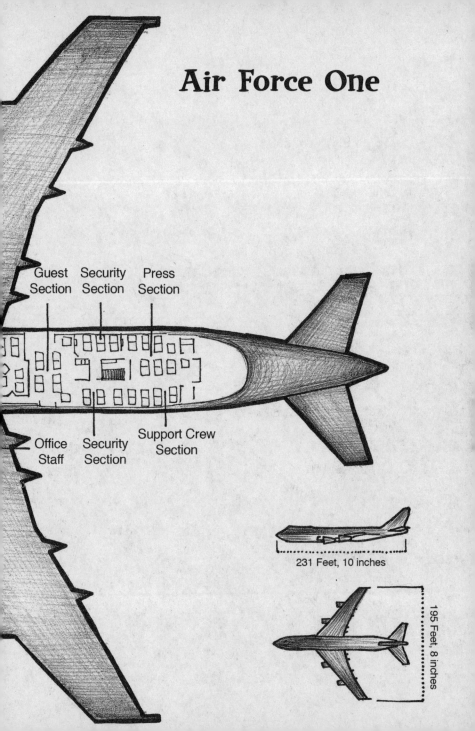

Air Force One

Guest Section

Security Section

Press Section

Office Staff

Security Section

Support Crew Section

231 Feet, 10 inches

195 Feet, 8 inches

Gregory's birthday is filled with surprises!
Read on for a sneak peek.

★ ★ ★ ★ ★ ★ ★ ★ ★ ★

Mice don't have a good history when it comes to surprises. Here's a list of reasons why:

1. Mousetraps
2. Pest control
3. Predators
4. Fire

Of course, these are all *bad* surprises. Sometimes mice have good surprises. Like when the baker makes a small mistake. Those treats go into the trash. This means it's sugar time for the Squeakertons, a mouse family that has eaten White House food for over two hundred years.

And birthdays! Birthdays are the best way to surprise somebody. Mr. James F. Squeakerton, the sort-of mouse president, asked his wife, Vivian, to marry him on her birthday. She got to smash open a piñata. Inside, she found candy *and* a wedding ribbon. (Mice don't wear rings on their claws. That would be weird.)

The Squeakerton mice have a very special celebration planned on Presidents' Day. Presidents' Day falls on a different day every year, and this year, it happens to be on Gregory Squeakerton's birthday. Gregory is the bodyguard for James F. Squeakerton's children, Ava and Dean. Gregory makes sure those little mice stay out of trouble. Most of the time.

Something else you should know about Gregory: he loves history. He is very proud to live in the White House. He can tell you anything you want to know about the White House. Probably even things you don't want to know. Like, did you know it takes 570 gallons of paint to cover the White House. See? Not a very useful fact (unless you're a painter).

Yes, the Squeakerton family wanted to celebrate the wonderful leaders they'd watched throughout the years. But they also really wanted to make the day unforgettable for Gregory.

There were just three problems:

1. Mice like Gregory don't like surprises. Gregory plans out his whole day, from his breakfast menu to his bathroom breaks. There's no room for surprises in his schedule.
2. C-a-t-s *love* surprises. They also love messing up surprises for other animals. C-a-t-s are evil. You probably already knew that, but mice think it's important to remind you.

3. Humans run the show in the White House. And sometimes human plans mess up mouse plans. Not that humans have any idea about that. Those guys really only pay attention to themselves.

New friends. New adventures. Find a new series...just for you!

FOR THE SPORTS FAN

FOR THE ADVENTURER

FOR THE SUPERSTAR

FOR THE DREAMER

FOR THE ANIMAL LOVER

FOR THE EXPLORER

Illustrations (from left to right): © Mark Meyers; © Mike Boldt; © Brigette Barrager; © Qin Leng; © Russ Cox; © Wesley Lowe

RandomHouseKids.com